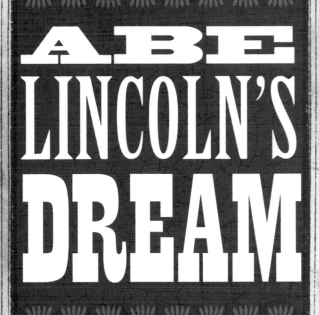

ABE LINCOLN'S DREAM

LANE SMITH

ROARING BROOK PRESS

NEW YORK

|1968| Neither would *Yuki.*

|1985| Or *Rex.*

Some said THEY SAW THE GHOST ON THE TWELFTH OF FEBRUARY. BUT ON THAT DAY, EVERYONE WAS WEARING STOVEPIPE HATS SO WHO COULD TELL?

A **GIRL** WANDERING FROM HER TOUR DISCOVERED
A TALL MAN STANDING OVER THE GETTYSBURG ADDRESS.

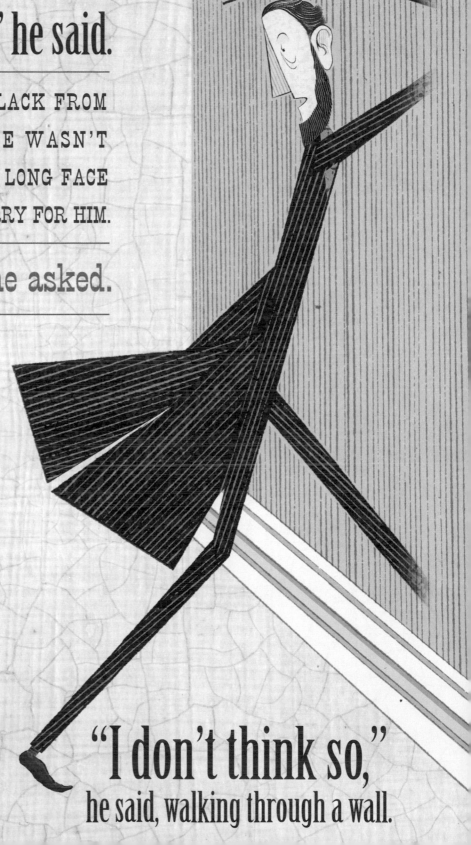

"Hi," said Quincy.

"HELLO, child," he said.

HE WAS DRESSED IN BLACK FROM
HAT TO BOOT, BUT SHE WASN'T
FRIGHTENED; HE HAD A LONG FACE
THAT MADE HER FEEL SORRY FOR HIM.

"Are you lost?" she asked.

"I don't think so,"
he said, walking through a wall.

"You look confused."

"**Why,** I'm right as rain," he said.

"**SURE?**"

"Well…not really…no. Ghosts are no good at telling fibs," he said. "You can see right through them."

"**That** is a **VERY SILLY** joke," she said.

"**Truth is,** I'm thinking of a dream I had last night," he said. "**It's always the same.** I'm on a ship sailing rapidly for some shore I know not where."

"**In my nightmares I'm in class,**" she said. "**Naked as a jaybird. Totally embarrassing.**"

"I wouldn't worry, that's a common dream," he said. "Like the one where bears have gotten into your cabin."

"You're tall," she said, taking four steps to his one.

"Do you know how LONG a man's legs should be?" he asked.

"NO."

"LONG enough to reach the floor."

SHE THOUGHT THIS JOKE WAS SILLIER THAN THE LAST, BUT SHE LAUGHED TO BE POLITE.

"I apologize if I appear restless but there was so much to do beyond 1865. Our union was so fragile, so uncertain. Like that ship on the rocky sea."

SHE LED HIM TO THE DOOR.

"**Oh no,** I never leave the Executive Mansion," he protested.

"You should," she said. "A lot has changed since 1865 . . .

"including the name of the Executive Mansion. We just call it the White House now."

THE GHOST DID THE
FLYING.

THE GIRL ANSWERED THE
QUESTIONS.

"And equality for all?" he asked.

"That's working out too," she said. "It's getting better all the time."

"But I think overall the founding fathers would
be proud of our progress, don't you?" said Quincy.

"WHY, I think they would be over the moon."

"OVER THE MOON, YES!

THERE'S ONE LAST THING I WANT TO SHOW YOU," she said.

"MY STARS,"

he said. "We HAVE come a long way.

THREE CHEERS AND
BALLYHOO!"

"KNOCK, KNOCK," she said.
"Who's there?" he said.
"ORANGE."
"ORANGE who?"
"ORANGE you feeling better now?"

HIS TOUR OVER, HE RETURNED HER TO HERS AS HE BEGAN TO **DISAPPEAR** **ONE** **FINAL** **TIME.**

School Buses

THAT NIGHT QUINCY HAD A DREAM.

She dreamed of a man, A TALL MAN IN BLACK, on a boat moving RAPIDLY toward the rising SUN.

"That is a VERY SILLY joke," he said.

HE WAS SMILING.

AFTERWORD

MR. LINCOLN'S DREAM

The morning of his assassination, April 14, 1865, President Lincoln was haunted by a dream from the night before. He told his cabinet members he had seen himself "In an indescribable vessel moving rapidly toward an indistinct shore." In fact, this was a dream the president had had several times, often before a momentous event.

PRESIDENTIAL POOCHES

The dogs featured in this book are Fala, the Scottish terrier of Franklin Delano Roosevelt (32nd president), Yuki, the mixed breed of Lyndon Johnson (36th president), and Rex, the Cavalier King Charles spaniel of Ronald Reagan (40th president), who drove the occupants of the White House crazy with his barking at the Lincoln Bedroom.

THIS BOOK IS DEDICATED TO SANDY WHO HAILS FROM THE LAND OF LINCOLN.

Published by Roaring Brook Press
Roaring Brook Press is a division of Holtzbrinck Publishing Holdings Limited Partnership
175 Fifth Avenue, New York, New York 10010

Library of Congress Cataloging-in-Publication Data
Smith, Lane.
   Abe Lincoln's dream / [written and] illustrated by Lane Smith. — 1st ed.
     p. cm.
   Summary: When a schoolgirl gets separated from her tour of the White House
and finds herself in the Lincoln bedroom, she also discovers the ghost of the great man himself.
   ISBN 978-1-59643-608-4 (hardcover)
   1. Lincoln, Abraham, 1809–1865—Juvenile fiction. [1. Lincoln, Abraham, 1809–1865—Fiction.
   2. White House (Washington, D.C.)—Fiction. 3. Ghosts—Fiction.] I. Title.
   PZ7.S6538Ab 2012
   [E]—dc23

2012020110

Roaring Brook Press books are available for special promotions and premiums.
For details contact: Director of Special Markets, Holtzbrinck Publishers.
First Edition 2012
Printed in the United States of America by Phoenix Color Corp. d/b/a Lehigh Phoenix, Hagerstown, Maryland
1 3 5 7 9 10 8 6 4 2

The illustrations were created with pen-and-ink, oil paint, and digital.

BOOK DESIGN BY MOLLY LEACH